MILLIONS OF CATS

BY WANDA GÁG

Coward-McCann   New York

Published by
COWARD-McCANN, INC.
51 Madison Avenue/New York, New York 10010

Copyright 1928 by Coward-McCann, Inc.;
renewal copyright © 1956 by Robert Janssen.
All rights reserved. This book, or parts thereof, may not
be reproduced in any form without permission in writing
from the Publishers.

First hardcover edition published September, 1928
First paperback edition published September, 1977

ISBN 0-698-20091-8 (hardcover trade edition)
ISBN 0-698-20434-4 (paperback edition)
Library of Congress Catalogue Card Number: 28-21571

PRINTED IN THE UNITED STATES OF AMERICA

Fifty-second Impression (hardcover trade edition)
Eighth Impression (paperback edition)

MILLIONS OF CATS

Once upon a time there was a very old man and a very old woman. They lived in a nice clean house which had flowers

all around it, except where the door was. But they couldn't be happy because they were so very lonely.

"If we only had a cat!" sighed the very old woman.

"A cat?" asked the very old man.

"Yes, a sweet little fluffy cat," said the very old woman.

"I will get you a cat, my dear," said the very old man.

And he set out over the hills to look for one. He climbed over the sunny hills. He trudged through the cool valleys. He walked a long, long time and at last he came to a hill which was quite covered with cats.

Cats here, cats there,
Cats and kittens everywhere,
Hundreds of cats,
Thousands of cats,
Millions and billions and trillions of cats.

"Oh," cried the old man joyfully,
"Now I can choose
the prettiest
cat and take
it home with
me!" So he
chose one.
It was white.
But just
as he was a-
bout to leave,
he saw anoth-
er one all
black and white
and it seemed
just as pretty as the first.
So he took this one also.

But then he saw a fuzzy grey
kitten way over
here which was
every bit as
pretty as
the others
so he took
it too.

And now
he saw one
way down
in a cor-
ner which
he thought
too lovely to
leave so he took this too.

And just then, over here, the very old man found a kitten which was black and very beautiful. "It would be a shame to leave that one," said the very old man . So he took it.

And now, over there,
he saw a cat which had
brown and yellow stripes
like a baby tiger.
"I simply must take
it!" cried the very old
man, and he did.

So it happened that every time the very old man looked up, he saw another cat which was so pretty he could not bear to leave it, and before he knew it, he had chosen them all.

And so he went back over the sunny hills and down through the cool valleys, to show all his pretty kittens to the very old woman.

It was very funny to see those hundreds and thousands and millions and billions and trillions of cats following him.

They came to a pond.
"Mew, mew! We are thirsty!" cried the
Hundreds of cats,
Thousands of cats,
Millions and billions and trillions of cats.

"Well, here is a great deal of water,"
said the very old man.
  Each cat took a sip of water, and
the pond was gone!

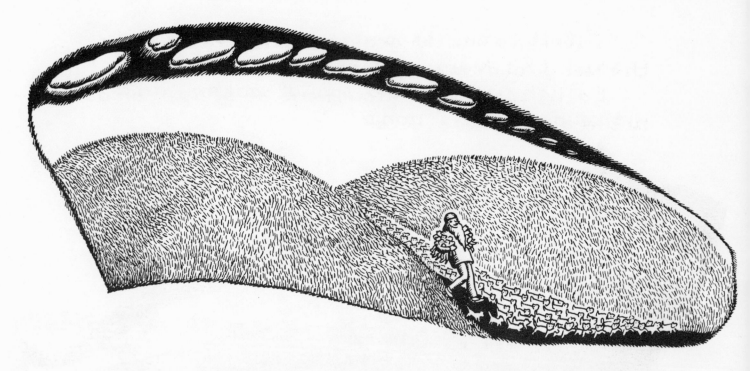

"Mew, mew! Now we are hungry!" said the
Hundreds of cats,
Thousands of cats,
Millions and billions and trillions of cats.

"There is much grass on the hills," said the very old man.

Each cat ate a mouthful of grass and not a blade was left!

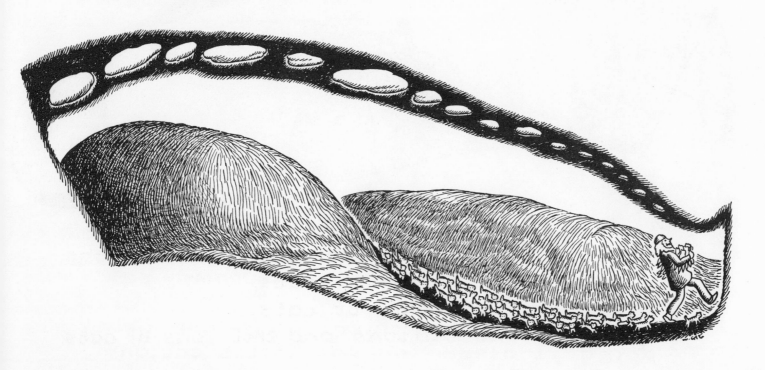

Pretty soon the very old woman saw
them coming.
"My dear!" she cried, "What are you
doing? I asked for one little cat, and
what do I see? —

" Cats here, cats there,
Cats and kittens everywhere,
Hundreds of cats,
Thousands of cats,
Millions and billions and trillions of cats.

"But we can never feed them all," said the very old woman, "They will eat us out of house and home."

"I never thought of that," said the very old man, "What shall we do?"

The very old woman thought for a while and then she said, "I know! We will let the cats decide which one we should keep."

"Oh yes," said the very old man, and he called to the cats, "Which one of you is the prettiest?"

"I am!"

"I am!"

"No, I am!"

"No, I am the prettiest!" "I am!"

"No, I am! I am! I am!" cried hundreds and thousands and millions and billions and trillions of voices, for each cat thought itself the prettiest.

And they began to quarrel.

They bit and scratched and clawed each other and made such a great noise that the very old man and the very old woman ran into the house as fast as they could. They did not like such quarreling. But after a while the noise stopped and the very old man and the very old woman peeped out of the window to see what had happened. They could not see a single cat!

"I think they must have eaten each other all up," said the very old woman, "It's too bad!" "But look!" said the very old man, and he pointed to a bunch of high grass. In it sat one little frightened kitten. They went out and picked it up. It was thin and scraggly.

"Poor little kitty," said the very old woman.

"Dear little kitty," said the very old man, "how does it happen that you were not eaten up with all those hundreds and thousands and millions and billions and trillions of cats?"

"Oh, I'm just a very homely little cat," said the kitten," So when you asked who was the prettiest, I didn't say anything. So nobody bothered about me."

They took the kitten into the house, where the
very old woman gave it a warm bath and brushed
its fur until it was soft and shiny.

Every day they gave
it plenty of
milk—

—and soon it grew
nice and
plump.

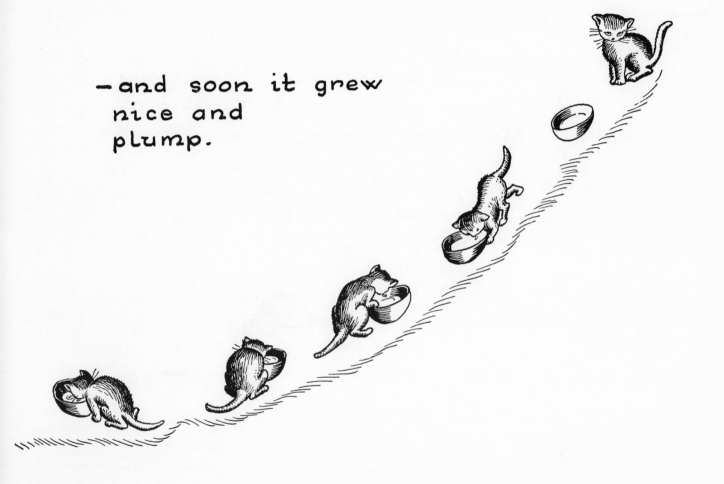

And it is a very pretty cat, after all!" said the very old woman.

"It is the most beautiful cat in the whole world," said the very old man. "I ought to know, for I've seen—
Hundreds of cats,
Thousands of cats,
Millions and billions and trillions of cats—
and not one was as pretty as this one."